"The new kid is weird," Richard says as he and Gavin and Carlos make their way to the foursquare court. Carlos has the ball and is ahead of Richard and Gavin, dribbling as he goes.

"Really weird," Gavin agrees.

"And I don't believe that he's been to ten schools. He'd be changing schools all the time."

"Yeah," Carlos calls over his shoulder. "He's lying."

The three boys look at Khufu, who's sitting on a bench, reading a book. A book! Who reads a book during recess?

THE CARVER CHRONICLES

— BOOK FIVE —

THE NEW KID

BY Karen English

ILLUSTRATED BY
Laura Freeman

Houghton Mifflin Harcourt · Boston · New York

The text was set in Napoleone Slab.

The Library of Congress has cataloged the hardcover edition as follows:
Names: English, Karen, author. | Freeman, Laura (Illustrator), illustrator.
Title: The new kid / by Karen English ; illustrated by Laura Freeman.
Description: Boston ; New York : Clarion Books, [2017] |
Series: The Carver Chronicles ; book five | Summary: "Third-grader Gavin and
his friends aren't sure what to make of the new boy in their class, Khufu.
He doesn't look or act like other kids. When Gavin's bike goes missing, they
think Khufu stole it, but did he?" — Provided by publisher.
Identifiers: LCCN 2017003167 | ISBN 9781328703996 (hardcover)
Subjects: | CYAC: Lost and found possessions—Fiction. | Friendship—Fiction.
| Schools—Fiction. | African Americans—Fiction. | BISAC: JUVENILE
FICTION / People & Places / United States / African American. | JUVENILE
FICTION / Social Issues / Friendship. | JUVENILE FICTION / Humorous
Stories. | JUVENILE FICTION / Social Issues / Bullying. | JUVENILE FICTION
/ Social Issues / Peer Pressure. | JUVENILE FICTION / Readers / Chapter
Books.
Classification: LCC PZ7.E7232 New 2017 | DDC [Fic]—dc23
LC record available at https://lccn.loc.gov/2017003167

ISBN: 978-1-328-70399-6 hardcover
ISBN: 978-1-328-49797-0 paperback

Printed in the United States of America
DOC 10 9 8 7 6 5 4 3
4500779824

For Gavin, Jacob, Isaac, and Idris

— K.E.

To Milo, an honest critic and a patient model

— L.F.

• Contents •

One
New Boy

There is a new boy in Room Ten. At least, Gavin thinks the person is a boy. This person has on boy clothes and a boy shirt, but his hair is in two cornrow braids that hang down the back. He's thin and short. Well, shorter than Gavin. And he has a piercing stare. He could be a girl. But the jeans are definitely boy jeans. So he's a boy, and now he's just sitting there, looking around, with his chin resting on his palm.

The students finish putting their things in their cubbies and settle down to tackle the morning journal topic, "My Weekend." Gavin wonders, *Why is the topic always "My Weekend" on Monday mornings? Is Ms. Shelby-Ortiz seriously interested in our weekends? Isn't there enough to think about with her own weekend?*

Ms. Shelby-Ortiz steps to the front of the class. Though no one is talking, she puts her forefinger to her mouth and looks around with a bright, cheerful expression on her face. *Oh, no!* Gavin thinks. *Another one of her happy announcements where she's the only one who's excited.* Are they going to get five more minutes of recess? Now, that would be exciting. It's probably something like getting a salad bar in the cafeteria. His mom was excited when her job at the train station put a salad bar in the employees' cafeteria. She talked about it for weeks.

"Class, we have a new student joining us today!"

All eyes swivel to the kid sitting in the chair beside Ms. Shelby-Ortiz's desk. Everyone stares. He stares back. Then Ms. Shelby-Ortiz motions for him to join her at the front of the class. Slowly he pulls himself out of the chair and makes his way to her side. He stands there with a blank look on his face and his chin raised. *A strange look,* Gavin thinks.

"I'd like to introduce you to Khufu Grundy. He's going to be joining our class today."

Gavin puzzles over the name. He's never heard of

anyone having *Khufu* for a name. It sounds like a boy name, though.

Immediately Deja throws her head back and frowns. She whispers, "What kind of name is Khufu Grundy?" Then she's waving her hand all around until Ms. Shelby-Ortiz looks over at her and says, "Yes, Deja?"

"What kind of name is *Khufu?*" she blurts out.

Ms. Shelby-Ortiz looks puzzled. Khufu steps forward and says in a high-pitched voice, "Khufu is the name of the Egyptian Pharaoh that had the Great Pyramid of Giza built."

Deja's frown deepens, and she glances at Rosario beside her.

Ms. Shelby-Ortiz says, "Ahh. Class, we've seen the pyramids—in the book Erik brought to share. Remember?"

The room is quiet. Gavin remembers the book,

plus he's seen a TV program about some pyramids somewhere far away. Then the new kid pipes up in that little mouse voice again. "Khufu was actually the second Pharaoh of the Fourth Dynasty in Egypt."

"That's very interesting, Khufu, but can you tell us a little bit about yourself?" Ms. Shelby-Ortiz asks brightly.

"What would you like to know?"

Ms. Shelby-Ortiz seems a little surprised. Then she says, "Well, tell us about your old school and what you like to do for fun—hobbies, stuff like that. Do you have brothers and sisters?"

"I'll take your last question first, if you don't mind."

Some of the kids turn to look at one another.

"Sure," Ms. Shelby-Ortiz says.

Khufu clears his throat. "Well, I don't have any brothers and sisters. I'm an only child. I don't live with my mother, either. She's an artist, and she lives in an artist colony in New Mexico."

Gavin sees that Nikki's mouth has dropped open. She looks amazed.

"So I live with just my father. My hobby is

reading—all subjects. I like thinking. That's what I like to do for fun."

Ms. Shelby-Ortiz steps forward slightly. "And what about your last school? Can you tell us something about it?"

"I've been to ten schools," he says with one eyebrow raised. "I liked my last school best. It was a school for geniuses. Everyone in my old school was a genius." At this point, Khufu looks around at Gavin's classmates as if he's deciding whether each kid is a genius or not. His eyes rest on Gavin for an extra few seconds.

"My, my!" Ms. Shelby-Ortiz exclaims. "A genius school. I must say, I've never heard of that kind of school before."

"Well, it's true," Khufu says. "If you don't believe me, you can just call my old school and ask them. They'll tell you. Oh, and I was born in Sweden, and I didn't even speak English until I came to this country."

"Ah," Ms. Shelby-Ortiz says. "Oh, that won't be necessary, Khufu. I don't need to call your old school."

Gavin glances around. Deja's frown has deepened. There are more puzzled looks.

"Hmm. A genius school," Ms. Shelby-Ortiz repeats. She begins to gather the books and supplies he'll need. She places what she has in his arms and tells him to take the empty seat next to Gavin.

"Gavin, raise your hand so he'll know where to sit."

Gavin raises his hand. Khufu turns and stares at him again. Then he shrugs and makes his way to the table. Gavin tries to ignore Khufu as he puts his books and journal on his desk and places his two brand-new, freshly sharpened pencils on the desktop, taking care to line them up next to each other.

Gavin goes back to his journal, noting that Khufu has opened up his own journal and, without hesitation, has begun to write and write as if he doesn't

even have to think first or take a small break to ponder some more.

He must have had a great weekend, Gavin decides. His own weekend was unexciting. His older sister, Danielle, who thinks she's so great because she's finally become a teenager, ratted on him about shoving his shoes, pajamas, dirty jeans, and socks under his bed and then declaring his room clean. She also told his parents that he took the last of the Oreos up to his room to eat before dinner, and that he was playing video games instead of reading like he was supposed to. *What a snitch.*

All because he tattled on her for bringing her phone to breakfast and texting under the table.

So he had to clean his room and read for an hour before he could go outside and shoot hoops, play with his new video game, or ride his brand-new bike over to his friend Richard's. It's a BMX—silver and blue. Ever since he got it for his birthday, he's been leaving it outside the garage so he can look out the window and stare at it and think, *That's my bike.*

As he's struggling to get all this in his journal, he continues to hear the fast scratchings of Khufu's pencil across his own journal page. It's almost as if Khufu's pencil can't keep up with his thoughts. Gavin looks over at him. He's hunched over his desk with a tense look on his face. What could he be writing?

● ● ●

"He's weird," Richard says as he and Gavin and Carlos make their way to the foursquare court. Carlos has the ball and is ahead of Richard and Gavin, dribbling as he goes.

"Really weird," Gavin agrees.

"And I don't believe that he's been to ten schools. He'd be changing schools all the time."

"Yeah," Carlos calls over his shoulder. "He's lying."

The three boys look at Khufu, who's sitting on a bench, reading a book. A book! Who reads a book at recess?

● ● ●

On Mondays, they have science at the end of the day— after math. This week, the students in Room Ten are working on their solar systems, made with Styrofoam balls, string, skewers, and coat hangers in different sizes. You can choose to hang the balls from a coat hanger or place them on skewers. Everyone is excited. The class loves the hands-on activities that go with science.

Ms. Shelby-Ortiz is going through all the safety rules again. It's a boring thing she does whenever they're working with materials: No sword fighting with the skewers—and be careful with them because one could get hurt by the pointed ends; be careful painting the Styrofoam balls (you're stuck with whatever mistakes you make). "What color are you painting Earth?" she poses, as if to trick them.

"Mostly blue for water, with brown for the landmasses," Antonia says without raising her hand and waiting to be recognized. Gavin notices Khufu staring at Antonia with a tiny frown and wonders what he's thinking. Khufu has a squint to his eyes.

"What about the biggest Styrofoam ball?"

"Yellow for the sun," several students offer.
Suddenly there's a shriek—coming from Nikki. She jumps up so fast, her chair topples over. "A spider!" she calls out, clutching her throat for some reason. Some

of the girls react similarly, jumping up and scooting their chairs back.

"You don't have to be afraid," Ms. Shelby-Ortiz says calmly. "It's not going to hurt you."

"But Ms. Shelby-Ortiz," Deja begins, sticking up for her friend, "it could be one of those poisonous spiders."

"Most spiders are harmless," Khufu informs the class, though no one asked him.

"Not the fiddler spider. Have you ever heard of the fiddler spider?" Rosario counters.

"It's also called the brown recluse, and of course I've heard of the brown recluse," Khufu says simply.

"Its bite can paralyze you. You won't be able to walk or even talk," Rosario declares.

At this, Khufu smiles ever so slightly.

"It can make your skin fall off," Richard calls out.

"No, it can't," Khufu replies.

Some of the kids laugh. Ms. Shelby-Ortiz, who's

just been watching this exchange, goes over to Nikki's desk and asks, "Where's the spider?"

"It got away," Nikki says.

"Good. Let's get back to work." She goes to the board and draws a circle. In the center, she writes, *Sun*. She draws nine concentric ovals around it. Then she calls on one kid after another to go up to the board and draw a planet on one of the ovals showing its size and its nearness to the sun. Everyone is eager to do this. All the kids in Ms. Shelby-Ortiz's class love to draw on the whiteboard.

When the solar system is completed and everyone is gazing at it proudly, Khufu raises his hand.

"Yes, Khufu?" Ms. Shelby-Ortiz says.

"Ms. Shelby-Ortiz, that solar system would be way more interesting if we put Pluto in the eighth position away from the sun. Because there are times when Neptune is ninth away from the sun. You see, Pluto's orbit around the sun is elliptical, and there are times when it crosses Neptune's orbit and becomes closer to the sun than Neptune. The last time was in 1979," he adds.

Ms. Shelby-Ortiz smiles as if she already knew this but didn't want to make things too complicated.

By then, a lot of kids are staring at Khufu intently. It was jarring enough when they learned that Pluto wasn't even a regular planet. That it was something called a *dwarf planet*—meaning way too small to be a regular planet. Now they had to picture Neptune kind of taking its place in the orbits.

"Very good, Khufu. I'm impressed," Ms. Shelby-Ortiz says—and he looks even more smug.

Two
After School

"I don't like him," Carlos says after school as the group—Carlos, Calvin, Richard, and Gavin—walks toward Delvecchio's market. That's where they go most days, to get candy and chips.

"He's a know-it-all," Richard says.

"And I've never even heard of a school for geniuses," Gavin adds. Then he thinks that if there were such a school, he, Gavin, probably would not be in it. He knows he isn't a *genius*. Though maybe he could learn to be. Was that possible? To learn to be a genius?

● ● ●

Gavin has a candy bar in his jacket pocket when he climbs the porch steps to his front door. If Danielle discovers he has candy, she'll tell their mother, and then his mother will give him a lecture about the damaging effects of too much sugar and how when he thinks he wants sugar, he should reach for an apple or an orange and satisfy his sugar craving that way. When his mother talks like that, he has to make himself look like he's really listening until she's finished. But he already knows he will not be substituting a candy bar with an apple. That's just not going to happen.

As he heads to the kitchen to get a glass of juice (though his mother would rather he get a glass of water), he notices his great-aunt Myrtle's suitcase at the bottom of the staircase. She's visiting again. This time she hurt her back, and once again his great-uncle Vestor is off to his Barbershop Harmonizers' Convention. It was all explained to him the night before, but he conveniently forgot. Until now.

Suddenly, there's Danielle standing in the doorway of the living room with her arms crossed.

"Aunt Myrtle's suitcase?" he asks. "I thought she was

coming tomorrow." Though she is Gavin's dad's aunt (and thus Gavin's great-aunt), the whole family refers to her as Aunt Myrtle.

Danielle smiles. Not a nice smile, but a smile that says, *I'm getting ready to tell you something that you're not going to like.* "She's already here."

"Where is she?" Gavin says, looking around.

"Upstairs in the guest bedroom."

"Already?"

"Yep."

"What about Carlotta?" Carlotta is Aunt Myrtle's dog.

"In the kennel."

"Why didn't she bring her?"

Danielle smiles more widely and says, "She didn't want to risk her getting lost. Like last time."

"But I found her!"

"Still. Anyway, she needs you to take her suitcase up to the guest room."

"Why can't you do it?"

Danielle snaps her fingers and rolls her neck. "Because it's a boy job," she says.

Gavin sighs and grabs the suitcase by the handle. It's surprisingly heavy, and he has to drag it up the steps. He's huffing and puffing by the time he rolls it into the guest bedroom.

His great-aunt Myrtle—or GAM, as he likes to think of her for short—is propped up in bed in a floral robe and with some kind of bonnet on her head.

"Hi, Aunt Myrtle," he says. "How are you doing?" He doesn't really want to know, but he's trying to be polite. He doesn't want her accusing him of being rude.

"Gavin, can you crack that open?" she says, nodding at the window across the room. "I'm about to burn up."

Gavin walks over, grabs the two handles at the bottom of the frame, and tugs. It seems to be stuck. He tugs harder and finally manages to jerk it open. He steps away and turns toward GAM. Instead of a grateful smile, she has a big frown on her face. "Well, my goodness. Are you trying to make me freeze to death? That's way too much."

With more tugs and heaves, somehow Gavin is able to lower it. He looks back over his shoulder to see if it's okay. GAM is shaking her head slowly, side to side. "Now you want to make the room like an oven."

Gavin sighs and manages to raise the window-pane just a few inches. "Is that okay?" he asks.

She shrugs. "It'll do."

He sighs again, but not so loudly that she can hear him. It's mainly in his head.

GAM pats the bed. "Now come on over here and tell me what you've been up to."

Gavin doesn't want to sit down next to GAM and tell her what he's been up to. He wants to go to the kitchen and get some chips before his mother gets home from her job at the train station. He wants to relax. Yet he sits on the foot of the bed and waits.

"So how have you been doing?"

"Fine," he says.

"How's school?" she asks, looking at him intently.

"Fine," he says.

"Are you getting good grades?"

"Uh-huh."

"What's your favorite subject?"

"Science."

"Mmm. Go get me a nice cup of tea. Would you?"

"Yes, Aunt Myrtle."

He doesn't sigh again until he's on the other side of the guest room door. Now his snack will be further delayed, which means his homework is going to be delayed, which means getting permission from his mom, who should be home from work any minute, to ride his bike over to Richard's after homework will be delayed.

He goes into the kitchen to put the teakettle on the burner, and there's his mother, carrying in a bag of groceries. She reaches into the bag, takes out an apple, and rinses it under the tap. "Here," she says, handing it to him.

He looks at the apple in his hand and tries not to frown at it.

"Oh, Gavin," his mother continues, "go see if Aunt Myrtle needs anything."

Once again, Gavin sighs inwardly. Then he has a

kind of sneaky idea. "I already know," he says. "She wants a cup of tea."

"Okay, I'll take care of that." His mother puts the kettle on and gets a mug out of the cabinet. While she stands beside the stove and starts to go through a stack of mail, Gavin is able to get the package of chocolate chip cookies out of the cabinet, pluck out three, and slip them into his pocket. He returns the package to the cabinet and almost tiptoes out of the kitchen.

"Wait," his mother says.

He stops. Did she see him? She picks up the apple he left on the counter. "You forgot your apple."

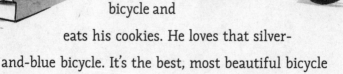

Gavin grabs the apple and finally eases out the back door onto the porch. He sits on the top step and looks at his new bicycle and eats his cookies. He loves that silver-and-blue bicycle. It's the best, most beautiful bicycle he's ever seen. Well, maybe not the most beautiful in the whole wide world, but it's the most beautiful one to Gavin.

● ● ●

After a while he gets up, returns to the kitchen, and places the apple in the fruit bowl with all the other apples. He settles at the table to start his homework. He doesn't want to chance doing it in his bedroom. He'd have to pass the guest room to get there, and Aunt Myrtle might see him and think of something else she wants him to do.

Three
Here Comes the Bike Squad

So the plan is for him, Richard, Carlos, and Calvin to ride their bikes to school the next day. Each boy has already promised his parents that he will be sure to ride with a helmet on.

They all had to promise that they would stay on the quiet side streets instead of the busy main roads, too. Gavin has never ridden his bike to school before. He can hardly contain his excitement.

● ● ●

In the morning, Gavin slips out of his bedroom and tiptoes past the guest room, hoping that Aunt Myrtle can't hear him. He's anxious to get started on his day. The last thing he needs is to be quizzed by GAM about chores and school and if he's being helpful and how he's doing. And he certainly doesn't want to go through that window-opening-and-closing thing again.

He slips into the bathroom and quickly brushes his teeth and runs a brush through his hair. Hoping he's out of her earshot, he dashes down the stairs, grabs his lunch from the refrigerator, downs a bowl of Cheerios while standing at the sink, and turns to head out the back door.

But his mother appears in the kitchen doorway with her arms crossed.

"Where do you think you're going?" she asks.

"I made up my bed, brushed my teeth, combed my hair, ate breakfast—*everything*. We're all meeting at Richard's and riding our bikes to school together." Surely his mother can't find fault with that.

"You have your helmet?"

"Yes."

"Don't you dare ride your bike without it."

"Okay," Gavin says, hoisting his backpack higher onto his shoulder.

"Come straight home after school."

"I will."

Finally he's released. He heads out the door toward

his beloved silver-and-blue bicycle from Wheel World. It's waiting for him right where he left it outside the garage. He grabs his helmet, which hangs from the handlebars, and slips it on. He adjusts his backpack, climbs onto his bike, and at last—he's off.

● ● ●

Biking with his friends toward Carver Elementary feels great. They stick to the side streets but still arrive at school much earlier than usual, which is actually not what Gavin had in mind. He'd pictured arriving when the playground was full of kids and all of them stopping their play to turn and stare at the bicycle brigade. But there are only a few students on the playground, and maybe only two or three notice Gavin and his friends.

There's no bike riding allowed on the playground, so they have to dismount and walk to the bicycle rack at the side of the building, next to the schoolyard gate.

Gavin's friends take their locks out of their backpacks and prepare to secure their bikes to the rack. It's only then that Gavin realizes *he forgot his!* While the others are locking their bikes to the rack, Gavin is just standing there, staring at his beautiful silver-and-blue bicycle.

"What's wrong?" Richard asks, putting the key to his lock in his pocket.

"I forgot my lock."

"Wow," Richard says. He frowns. Then he turns to the rest of the group. "Hey, Gavin forgot his lock."

"He should take his bike back home and get a ride to school," Carlos suggests.

"No. Then he'll be super late," Calvin says.

"Better to be late than get your bike stolen," counters Richard.

"You think my bike's going to get stolen?" Gavin asks.

"I think people going by will just think it's locked," Calvin says. "Or maybe one of us can lock our bike to Gavin's."

The boys study their own locks.

"They're not long enough," Carlos points out.

Gavin positions his bike between Carlos's and Richard's, hoping everyone will just assume all the bikes are locked. He and his friends walk toward Room Ten's lineup area. Gavin looks back at his bicycle with a pinch of dread. Then he tells himself that it will be all right. Nobody's going to steal his bike. Nobody's going to think that it's not locked.

○ ○ ○

Gavin repeats this to himself as he's putting his lunch and helmet away in his cubby. Happily, he's one of the students who are allowed to hang their backpacks on their chairs. Some kids don't have that privilege because they're constantly going in their bags for small toys or snacks. Those are the ones who must keep their backpacks in their cubbies.

He takes his seat at his table and checks the whiteboard for the morning journal topic. It's open, he's relieved to see. He gets to write about anything he chooses. He's going to write about his bike. Yes, his bike! He thinks of it sitting out there in the rack all silvery and gleaming. His bicycle.

He looks over at the weird new boy's empty seat and momentarily wonders where he is—Khufu. Then he gets to work on today's journal entry.

I'm feeling pretty happy today, Morning Journal, because I worked really hard and I was able to get me a new bike for my birthday. I'm so happy. I had to get 100s on my spelling tests for a month. I had to not argue with my sister, Danielle. And she's really hard to not argue with because she likes to argue and pick on me and try to make things hard for me, like she'll tell on me if I don't clean my room the way my mother wants and she'll tell on me if I might sneak in one video game when I'm supposed to be reading. Stuff like that. So I had to go a long time and not argue. Plus I had to do all my chores without being reminded. Take the trash out, take the cans to the curb, make my bed, put all dirty clothes in the hamper, do my homework. Oh, and now I have to be nice to Aunt Myrtle (she's my great-aunt, and I call her GAM—but not to her face), who's staying with us until Uncle Vestor comes back from his barbershop convention thing. Why do they have to have a convention about barbershop singing groups anyway? So I got my bike and I'm so happy. I will keep it forever and ride it forever because I see old people on bikes, especially at the lake. So I'm keeping my bike forever.

Ms. Shelby-Ortiz rings her bell when it's time to stop and says, "Put away your journals." Gavin is disappointed. He was hoping Ms. Shelby-Ortiz would call on a few kids to share what they've written. He wants the whole class to know how he feels about his bike. Now he's just waiting for recess so he can check on it. So he can make sure his bike is still in the bike rack—*with no lock*.

Khufu comes in late while the class is doing silent reading and Ms. Shelby-Ortiz is sitting at her desk grading papers. He puts away his lunch and heads toward his desk at Gavin's table.

"Khufu," Ms. Shelby-Ortiz says, "why are you late?"

Khufu, who has just sat down, stands up to answer. *Why's he standing?* Gavin wonders.

"My father's car broke down in the middle of Ashby, and I had to walk the rest of the way. I didn't leave early enough to walk. I left early enough to be driven."

Ms. Shelby-Ortiz looks like she's stifling a smile. "I see," she says, and that's that.

● ● ●

The bell finally rings, and Gavin can't wait for his teacher to call his table to be dismissed for recess. Miraculously, she calls his first. Gavin and his tablemates march to the door like soldiers, form an extra-straight line, and wait for the other tables to be called. Then everyone has to wait for Richard to pick up bits of paper from the floor under his table. What's he doing with torn paper under his table, anyway?

He takes a long, long time cleaning up. Gavin has to hold himself back from tapping his foot, which probably wouldn't go over well with Ms. Shelby-Ortiz. He has to just stand there and wait.

Finally, everyone is in line and Ms. Shelby-Ortiz can let the class out with the same old words: "Walk. Don't run. And we have foursquare this week, and that's where I expect to find you when I come out at lineup time."

Every day. *Every day* she says the same thing while precious seconds of recess are lost. As soon as Gavin is outside, the class goes one way and Gavin goes another. He hurries toward the bike rack.

It's there. His bike, looking like it's just waiting for its rightful owner—him, Gavin. He can't wait to ride it home. He wants to go over to it and check it carefully, but the bike rack is off-limits during school hours, so he examines it from a distance. His heart has finally stopped beating fast, now that he's seen that his beautiful silver-and-blue bike is still there. Now he can run off and play in peace.

● ● ●

Later, when Ms. Shelby-Ortiz lets them out for lunch, Gavin does the same thing. His classmates go left, heading to the cafeteria or the lunch tables, and he goes right, to check the bike rack. *I will never leave my lock at home again,* he vows. *This is too nerve-racking.*

After lunch, the day drags. He checks the clock. Dismissal seems a hundred years away. He thinks of his bike. Is it missing him? He knows that's a crazy thing to think.

While the students are at their desks getting ready for math, Ms. Shelby-Ortiz has them form pairs to quiz each other on their multiplication facts. Khufu turns to Gavin and stares at him. Which means, Gavin guesses, he'll have to be Khufu's partner. He pulls his fact sheet out of his desk and deliberately starts with the sevens.

Of course Khufu knows all of his sevens. His eights, too. And nines. Gavin's not even surprised. Then it's his turn. Khufu quizzes Gavin, and he can

hardly get anything right. Sevens are his weakness. He knows only seven times seven and seven times ten, actually.

Soon, it's time for the actual quiz. Ms. Shelby-Ortiz tells the class to take out a piece of paper, head it, and number it from one to twenty. Khufu does this quickly, then sits tapping his pencil on his desk—waiting. Gavin thinks, *Genius school.*

Ms. Shelby-Ortiz begins calling out problems, and Khufu seems to write the answers without even having to think. He does something Gavin finds super annoying. Each time Khufu writes his answer, he taps his pencil and looks at Gavin while Gavin's still trying to think of the answer. Gavin wonders why he does that. Maybe it's to show what a genius he is.

Gavin has no problems with the fives and twos, but for most of the rest, he has to quickly guess. He knows he needs to study. *More.*

As soon as they turn in their quizzes, Khufu raises his hand. "Ms. Shelby-Ortiz, I have to leave early today. I have a dentist appointment. And my dad is already here. I saw him in the hall outside the attendance office."

Ms. Shelby-Ortiz frowns. "Why didn't you say something?"

Khufu doesn't answer her. Instead he says, "I have a note." Before Ms. Shelby-Ortiz can say anything, he's out of his seat and bringing it up to her.

She unfolds the note and reads it. Then she scrunches her mouth to the side like she's thinking. "Did you change the time on this?" she asks, looking down at Khufu. "It looks like it's supposed to be at three. Your appointment. But that's been scratched out and two o'clock is written over it."

"The dentist's receptionist did that—not me.

Someone else had the three o'clock appointment. So she had to give me the two o'clock appointment. And my father's already here," Khufu adds quickly.

"Stop in the office and show them your appointment slip."

"I will," he says. Then he grabs his backpack and hurries out.

Four
Dismissal, at Last

Finally, finally, *finally* the dismissal bell rings and Ms. Shelby-Ortiz begins her usual routine of looking for a table that seems "ready." Table Three, where Antonia sits, outshines Gavin's table, and they get to line up at the door first. Then Ms. Shelby-Ortiz looks carefully at the rest of them. She calls Carlos's table next. It's all Gavin can do to keep himself still and standing straight like a soldier behind his chair. He takes in a deep breath and waits.

His table is next, and he fast-walks to the line at the door. They can't leave until everyone is lined up, and Rosario is delaying everything by not keeping her stupid mouth shut. She's in the middle of a spat with Beverly over her Hello Kitty pencil. Beverly claims she *loaned* the pencil to Rosario, and Rosario says Beverly *gave* it to her.

Ms. Shelby-Ortiz walks over to their table, plucks the pencil out of Rosario's hand, and puts it away in her desk drawer. "You're holding up the class. We'll settle this tomorrow."

Gavin could hug Ms. Shelby-Ortiz then. Sometimes she seems to know just what to do.

"Class dismissed," she finally says, and Gavin fast-walks out of there. Once he's rounded the side of the school building, he breaks into a run toward the bike rack.

As soon as it is in sight, he stops. He blinks a few times. Where's his bicycle? Where's his shiny new silver-and-blue bicycle? He blinks again and walks slowly toward the bike rack. It's not there! Richard and the others come up behind him. The four of them stand there staring at the empty slot that once held Gavin's bicycle.

Richard asks the obvious. "Where's your bike?"

Gavin can't speak. His throat feels as if it's closing. He has to keep swallowing. He can't stop blinking. Finally, he squeezes out, "I don't know." Then he looks

up and down the street as if he might see someone riding by on his bike—by mistake. The street is clear, both ways. Calvin, Richard, and Carlos unlock their bikes and hang their helmets on the handlebars. Gavin's helmet dangles from his hand. He looks at it. What does he need that for? He's got no bike.

They start for Gavin's house, walking their bicycles to be in solidarity with him. Gavin barely notices. He's in shock. "Someone stole my bike," he says finally. Then he's quiet almost all the way home.

Richard breaks the silence with, "What are you going to do? Are you going to tell your dad?"

"I have to. He'll notice I don't have it."

"Your dad is going to feel sorry for you, probably."

"Not when he finds out that I forgot my lock. He'll say that I was irresponsible. Then he'll lecture me about money and being careless and on and on." Gavin feels tired just thinking about the lecture he's going to get. There will probably be a punishment, too.

● ● ●

Once they reach his house, his friends wave good-bye, mount their bikes, and ride off. Gavin watches them. Then he turns toward his front door. He knows

Danielle is behind that door somewhere. Once she gets a whiff of Gavin's carelessness, she'll go in search of their mother, who's off work on Tuesdays, to make the announcement. Maybe his mother will be kind of sympathetic. She's usually the sympathetic one. But Danielle will just be ready to spout off about the situation to their father as soon as he comes through the door. And GAM . . . He can just imagine the long lecture he'll get from her.

He goes around the side of the house and slips in through the back door. Of course Danielle's sitting at the kitchen table doing her homework. Couldn't she be doing that in her bedroom? She's eating a peanut butter and jelly sandwich while she's hunched over her math book. She licks her fingers and looks up at Gavin. "What's wrong, Gavmeister?"

What? Is it that obvious? He sighs. He might as well spill it, he decides. "Someone stole my bike."

She puts her sandwich down. Her eyes widen. Instead of jumping up and going in search of their mother to tattle, she asks, "What *happened?*" She seems genuinely concerned.

"I forgot my lock. So I couldn't lock it to the bike rack." Gavin's throat starts to ache again, and he feels his eyes filling with tears. He wipes them away quickly.

"Wow," she says. She frowns. "That's tough. Well, I have to let you know, you're probably going to be in for it. I predict big trouble."

Is she trying to make him feel better or worse?

"You need to think about how you're going to tell them." She shakes her head and takes a big bite out of her sandwich.

● ● ●

When Gavin gets to the top of the stairs, he tiptoes past the guest room, but the floorboard creaks under the carpet. "Is that you, Gavin?" he hears.

His shoulders slump. "Yes."

"Come on in here so I can look at you."

Gavin doesn't know what that means, but he does what GAM says.

"What's wrong?" she asks as soon as he's standing before her.

"Someone stole my bike." He says it quickly to get it over with.

"How did that happen?"

"I accidentally left my bike lock at home." He waits for her to fuss at him. But surprisingly, she doesn't.

"Oh, my. What did your mother say?"

Gavin sighs again. "I haven't told her yet."

"Best to get it over with. She's out in the garden. Go on. She might be very understanding."

She might be, but his dad isn't going to be. He is definitely going to give him a long lecture about responsibility and paying attention to what he is doing and not being careless. It is going to be bad.

His mother is coming through the back door and taking off her gardening gloves just as Gavin reaches the kitchen. He stops and stands there, looking down.

"What is it?" his mother asks. "Why are you looking like that?"

Gavin just continues to hang his head, hoping he's building up some sympathy in his mother.

"Spill it," she says in her no-nonsense voice.

Somehow it's harder than spilling it to Aunt

Myrtle. He takes in a deep breath and sighs once more. "My bike got stolen."

His mother frowns as if she doesn't fully understand what he just said. "What?"

"Someone stole my bike," says Gavin, and then he starts to cry and wipe his eyes at the same time.

"Sit down," his mother orders. She tears a paper towel off the roll and hands it to him to dry his tears. "Start at the beginning."

He explains that it wasn't until he got to school that he realized he didn't have his bike lock, and he thought it would be okay. His bike was there at recess, and he saw it there at lunchtime, too. But after school, it was gone. Someone took it.

In the middle of his explanation, his mother starts shaking her head. Then she sighs this big sigh and shakes her head some more. "Not good," she says. "You're going to have to tell your dad. He'll be home in about an hour. Right now, go do your homework."

○ ○ ○

At dinner, Danielle is watching him. Gavin can't tell if she has a pleased look on her face or a sympathetic one. But it doesn't matter. He decides to just blurt it out. "My bike got stolen," he says. Then he's afraid to look at his dad.

When he finally does, he's surprised to see a calm look on his father's face.

"How did that happen?"

Gavin tells him just what he told his mother. He watches his father's eyebrows slowly sink. "Let me get this straight. You forgot your bike lock? How?"

"Because we were all riding our bikes—Calvin, Richard, Carlos, and me."

"And I," his mother says, correcting him.

"And *I*," Gavin repeats. "So I was kind of excited, and I was concentrating on making sure I had my helmet and that I put it on, and . . ."

His father holds up a palm.

"Does he get another bike?" Danielle asks quickly.

"No, he doesn't get another bike. At least not any-time soon. However, he can start saving his allowance for one."

Gavin frowns. That's going to take a century.

"Being without your bike is going to be a nice little reminder to you about the consequences of careless-ness," his father says.

Gavin looks down.

"You don't even need to be punished," his mother adds. "It's probably going to be punishment enough to see all your pals with their bikes."

"So he doesn't get put on punishment?" Danielle asks.

"Is that your business?" GAM asks her with nar-rowed eyes.

"No," Danielle answers in a small voice.

"Then why don't you just stick to your own busi-ness?" GAM says, and Gavin could just hug her.

● ● ●

At least his mom drives him to school the next day so he doesn't have to walk alone and watch his friends ride by. He arrives before Richard, Carlos, and Calvin and goes directly to the bike rack to see if a miracle has occurred during the night and his bicycle is returned and sitting there waiting for him.

The rack is empty except for this really ugly orange bike that looks as if somebody spray-painted it and did a super-bad job. It's not even locked up, and Gavin can see why. No one would want that ugly thing anyway.

He's still staring at it when his friends pull up like a third-grade motorcycle gang.

"Whose bike?" Carlos asks, jumping off his own bicycle and rolling it toward the rack. Calvin and Richard are already locking up theirs.

"Yeah, whose bike?" Calvin asks.

"Sure is ugly," Richard says.

"It looks like it's been spray-painted," Calvin adds.

"But why that ugly orange?" asks Gavin.

"Kind of looks like your bike, Gavin, if it was silver and blue," Richard says. "Same extra-wide seat and everything."

"That was my mother's idea," Gavin informs his friends. "She said in the long run, it would be more comfortable."

"Same crisscross spokes, too," Calvin notes. "Just like yours. Except for the color."

Gavin studies it some more. "Yeah," he says slowly. It does kind of look like his bicycle.

"Wouldn't it be funny if that was really your bike and the person who stole it thought that just spray-painting it would fool everyone?" Richard asks.

Gavin is wondering the same thing. What if that orange bike is really his silver-and-blue bike? *Spray-painted orange.*

But before he can say anything, the lineup bell rings and the four of them head toward Room Ten's designated area.

● ● ●

For some reason, the picture of the orange bicycle just pops into Gavin's head during independent reading. There was something about that bike. It kind of looked like a BMX. Like his. Plus, a BMX is a great bike. Why would anyone want to spray-paint it orange unless they were trying to disguise it? Could that bike really be his? No, he decides. He's just doing some wishful thinking.

At recess, while his friends run to the foursquare court, Gavin looks over at the bicycle rack. He can see the orange bike, and now he studies it some more. It does have a similar seat. And there are those same spokes. And—it's definitely a BMX. But the ugly orange color . . . He frowns and turns toward the foursquare court. He notices Khufu sitting on the bench in the lunch area, reading, as usual. Gavin doesn't understand. Why is Khufu reading a book? Doesn't he like to play? Maybe that's what everyone did in genius school. Gavin makes his way over to his friends.

● ● ●

Later, while they all stand in line waiting for Ms. Shelby-Ortiz, he tells Carlos, who's standing right behind him, that he plans to find out who owns the orange bike because he's thinking it just might be . . . *his*.

Carlos's eyes widen. "I've been thinkin' that too. That bike looks just like yours, only spray-painted orange. I mean, for real. But how are you going to do that?" he asks.

"I'll figure something out."

● ● ●

And he does. Just before the dismissal bell rings, Gavin raises his hand and asks to go to the bathroom. He puts a look of urgency on his face and kind of wiggles in his seat.

"You may go *this* time," Ms. Shelby-Ortiz tells him. "But take your backpack with you, since it's so close to dismissal." Then she decides to make this a teaching moment. She stands up behind her desk, where she's been recording their math quiz scores, and says, "Who can tell me what morning recess and lunch recess are for?"

Sheila Sharpe's hand shoots up. Ms. Shelby-Ortiz calls on her.

"Both are so we can get exercise, because kids are getting fatter and fatter because they don't get enough exercise."

A few kids look over at Yolanda, who happens to have a few extra pounds on her. Yolanda frowns a little and looks down at her hands.

"Yes, we all need exercise, but what else?" Ms. Shelby-Ortiz asks.

"So we can eat our lunch, and morning recess is for snacks," calls out Ralph.

Ms. Shelby-Ortiz sighs because he didn't raise his hand first, but she seems to let it go. "Yes, and there's one more thing," she says.

Antonia is the only one who raises her hand.

"Antonia?" Ms. Shelby-Ortiz says.

"It's also for taking care of our restroom needs."

"You are so right, Antonia. Nicely put," Ms. Shelby-Ortiz says, looking like she wants to maybe laugh a little. She turns to Gavin. "I'll let you go this time, but from now on, please take care of your *restroom needs* during one of the two recesses."

Five
The Owner of the Orange Bike Is . . .

Finally, with backpack in tow, Gavin leaves while the rest of the class cleans up in preparation for the last bell.

He heads straight for the big trash bin on the side of the main building. From the far side of the bin, he has a good view of the bike rack. All he has to do is watch to see who claims the orange bicycle. If he had waited for the regular dismissal bell, the owner could have gotten to the rack and ridden off before Gavin even arrived.

Sure enough, lots of students are let out before any of Room Ten's kids. Ms. Shelby-Ortiz is probably making the class finish cleaning up before they can go. Stuff like straightening the library corner, taking stray papers out of their desks to put in the recycle bin, making sure all the mancala pieces have been returned to the box and all the markers in the can in the center of the table have their tops on. Irritating stuff like that. Made even more irritating when you just want to be dismissed already.

Of course Gavin recognizes his friends' bikes. And he knows which one belongs to Gregory Johnson (who's in the fifth grade). He recognizes Gregory Johnson's friend Paul Michaels's bike. And the one that belongs to this other fifth-grader named Thomas Murphy.

One by one, Gregory, Paul, and Thomas make it over to the rack, unlock their bicycles, slip on their helmets, and ride off. That leaves just Gavin's friends' bikes and the super-ugly orange one.

Gavin waits and wonders if anyone can see him. He steps back behind the trash bin until he hears the fast footsteps of someone approaching the bike rack. Someone who sounds like he's in a hurry. Gavin chances a peek. *Khufu?* Khufu is the owner of the orange bicycle?

Hmm. Maybe Khufu didn't really have to leave class early the day before for that dental appointment. That dental appointment might have been fake! Maybe Khufu just wanted to get out early so he could take Gavin's unlocked bicycle.

Khufu probably changed the time on his dentist's appointment slip himself. He needed some time to get the bike and get out of there before the dismissal bell. It was *Khufu. The new kid stole his bike!*

Now Khufu's backing the orange bicycle away from the rack, jumping on it, and riding away—*without a helmet*. Gavin is momentarily amazed. Khufu has no helmet and seems to feel fine. But aren't helmets the law? Can't Khufu get arrested for being on a bike without one? Ha! That would serve that thief right! He hopes a police officer sees Khufu and hauls him off to jail.

Gavin comes out from behind the trash bin, and

by the time Richard, Carlos, and Calvin show up, he's pacing next to their bicycles. "What took you guys so long?"

Carlos groans. "Ms. Shelby-Ortiz did a surprise desk check and had us take everything out of our desks and put all the stuff back in again—neatly. Oh, and we had to put all stray papers in the recycle bin, and Rosario found the hair ornament she accused Beverly of taking, and then we had to listen to this boring lecture about accusing people falsely."

"So where's the orange bike?" Richard asks.

"With *Khufu*," Gavin says simply.

"That's Khufu's bike?" Carlos asks.

"No, it's *my* bike, painted orange."

Calvin shakes his head. "You can't be sure."

Gavin feels himself waver. Then he says with fresh certainty, "It's a BMX like mine, and—"

"Gregory Johnson has a BMX, and so does his friend Thomas. The one in Mr. Willis's class," Carlos reminds him.

"Their bikes are way bigger," Gavin counters.

"Not *way* bigger. Just bigger," Carlos says. "And anyway, a lot of kids have BMXs."

Gavin turns to Carlos. "But they don't paint their BMXs *orange*. It's my bike. I know it is—even though he's tried to disguise it. I know it's my bike, and I have to get it back."

"How you plan on doing that?" Richard asks while slipping on his helmet.

"I'm thinking," he replies, noticing that Carlos and Calvin have slipped on their helmets as well. Soon he'll be left behind to walk home alone. He *has* to get his bike back. He *has* to come up with a plan.

Gavin watches his friends ride off. Then, just as he's starting up the street toward home, he hears a horn honk behind him. It's his mother. She must have decided that she didn't want him to walk home alone. She's kind of overprotective that way. Gavin sighs. He's gotta think of something. He can't have her picking him up every day like he's some kind of *baby* while his friends ride off on their cool bikes.

He sighs again as he gets into the back seat. His

mother turns and smiles at him just like he's her little baby boy.

● ● ●

When Gavin's mom pulls into the driveway, Gavin is surprised to see his friends sitting on his front porch. "You have homework to do, Gavin, and I'm sure your friends have homework as well," she says as she gets out of the car. "Don't be long." She greets the boys and goes into the house.

"What's going on?" Gavin asks.

"We have a plan," Richard says. "To get your bike back."

Gavin looks at the open windows and thinks of Danielle. "Let's go up to my room," he says. They walk their bikes around the side of the house and leave them lined up on the lawn before following him through the kitchen door.

Gavin leads his friends upstairs. Carlos and Richard flop down on his bed, and Calvin starts fiddling with the model airplane that once belonged to Gavin's dad but now sits on his dresser.

"Be careful with that," Gavin warns Calvin.

"This is what we're going to do," Richard says. "We're going to take the bike back."

There's silence. Then Gavin says, "How are we going to do that?"

"We just have to find out where Khufu lives, then see where he's keeping your bike," Richard explains. "So tomorrow I'll follow him home but make it so he doesn't notice."

Gavin feels uneasy for some reason. "How are you going to do that?"

"I'll just ride slow. But I'll keep him in view. He won't even know I'm behind him. Then, after that, we can just go back and get it, like on Saturday or something. Early."

"But how are we going to ride our bikes over there and get the bike too?" Calvin asks. "That'll be too many bikes."

They all fall quiet, thinking. "Gavin and I will do it. We'll just walk over there early Saturday morning," Richard says. "Gavin, you have to spend the night at my house."

Again Gavin feels a strange uneasiness. Then he pictures his bike—all painted over in that awful orange. "Okay. It's a plan," he agrees.

His friends leave, and he's about to head downstairs for a snack before starting his homework when Aunt Myrtle calls his name. He approaches her room with dread.

She starts in right away. "I couldn't help overhearing you and your friends' little scheme about getting your bike back, and I have a question for you."

She peers at him over her glasses. Gavin notices needlepoint on her lap. His mother sometimes does needlepoint—to relax, she says. "Now, what makes you think that child's bike is your bike?"

"I know it's mine," Gavin says.

"Because?"

"Because it's the same type—BMX—and it's the same size. They come in different sizes. It also has that fat seat Mom made me get—and it looks like it's been spray-painted this color I've never seen bikes come in before. And it has the same type of spokes that are really different-looking . . ." Gavin trails off, running out of similarities.

"Well, let me ask you this," Aunt Myrtle says. "Could all that be true and it still not be your bike?"

Gavin thinks hard. "It's my bike," he says after a moment. But then he wonders a tiny bit. Deep down inside.

"Mmm," she says. "You think about that." She goes back to her needlepoint, and Gavin is finally dismissed.

The orange bike sits in the rack when Gavin gets to school the next day. Gavin stares at it. It seems to be mocking him with its strange color and uneven paint job showing some places more orange than others—like it was done in a hurry. It looks like a bike that's been *disguised*. Carlos and Richard ride up then. The three of them stand there, staring at the bicycle.

"Yeah, that's your bike, all right," Carlos says, nodding. "I'm sure of it."

"Remember, I'm going to follow him today after school," Richard adds. "To see where he lives. Then me and Gavin can just go get it back."

Gavin and Richard nod. Then Gavin remembers what Aunt Myrtle said, and that funny feeling comes over him again.

Six
GAM's Thoughts

The day starts off like any other Thursday. Except it's the day Richard is going to find out where Gavin's bike is. As usual, Khufu scribbles nonstop in his morning journal and Gavin wonders what on earth he could be writing. Gavin's topic is about his stolen bike and how he felt when he first realized it was gone. And how it was kind of unbelievable at first. And how he kept staring and staring at the empty space where he'd put his bike that morning, because its emptiness just didn't seem real.

But now he knows there's a chance to get it back. He feels a flutter of excitement. He doesn't write that in his journal, or who he thinks stole his bicycle, since the culprit is sitting right next to him, all innocent and stuff. Gavin could drop his morning journal, and Khufu could pick it up and see his name in it. So Gavin keeps Khufu's name out of his writing. He just keeps Khufu's name in his head. He knows who he suspects, and all his friends know, too.

● ● ●

After school, there's his mother sitting in her car with the motor idling. Gavin has a miserable thought. What if his mother has to pick him up and drop him off all the way through high school? He supposes lots of kids are dropped off and picked up by their mothers until they're old enough to drive, but still, he'd rather imagine himself on his blue-and-silver bike, riding with his friends. Until he gets a car.

Suddenly Richard, Carlos, and Calvin are beside him, straddling their bikes. "I'll let you know what I find out," Richard says. "Then we can go early Saturday morning—really early—and get it."

"What if he comes out and catches you?" Calvin says.

"That's why we have to do it early, while everyone is still asleep," Gavin explains, trying to sound more sure of himself than he feels.

"You could get caught. Maybe by his *father*," Carlos says, his eyes big. "And what if the bike is locked?"

"Everything is going to work out," Richard says. "I have a feeling."

"There he is," Carlos announces. They all follow Carlos's pointing finger to watch Khufu take the bike out of the rack, climb onto it, and start down the street.

"See you," Richard says. He waits a bit, then starts down the street behind Khufu. Far behind.

Gavin climbs into the back seat of his mother's car and says, "Mom, can I spend the night at Richard's on Friday?" He knows Saturdays are chore days. All morning he cleans his room and sweeps the back porch and front porch and does whatever his mother thinks up. But maybe just this once.

"We'll see," his mother says.

That gives him hope. He's relieved that his parents seem to think being without his bike is punishment enough. He's counting on them to continue thinking like that. Now he remembers what spending the night at Richard's is like and wonders if it will be noisy again. Richard has three loud brothers who are always punching one another and arguing over the television or loudly playing video games.

● ● ●

His mother has groceries in the back of the car, and when she pulls into their driveway, she asks Gavin to help her carry them into the house. If there's one thing Gavin hates to do it's help carry groceries into the house. The second thing he hates is putting them away and seeing almost no snack food. There are no chips or candy or frozen pizzas.

GAM is in the kitchen, sitting at the table with a cup of tea. Her back has healed enough so that she can come downstairs now. *Maybe she can go home,* he thinks, and then chides himself for thinking it. It hasn't been so bad having her around these last few days. In fact, he likes GAM better now than when she was here before with Carlotta, her little Pomeranian.

"Hi, Aunt Myrtle."

She nods. "Hello, Gavin."

When the groceries are put away and his mother

has gone upstairs, GAM says, "And how was your day at school?" She looks at him over her glasses, waiting.

"Fine."

"Was your little friend at school?"

Gavin frowns. "Which one?"

"The one with the funny name. Gugu?"

"His name is Khufu and he was there, but he's not really my friend."

"Did you ask him about your bike?" she asks, taking a sip of tea.

"No, because he would only . . ." Gavin hesitates. He remembers his mother telling him that when she was a little girl, she was not allowed to say the word *lie*. She had to say *fib* or *tell a story*.

". . . tell a fib," Gavin says. "He tells *fibs* all the time. Stuff like he was born in Sweden and only spoke Swedish until he came to this country and that he's gone to ten schools and his last school was just for geniuses. He lives with only his father. That part is probably true."

GAM chuckles. "Now, that sure is an interesting character."

"And a thief," Gavin adds, thinking of the plan to get his bike back.

"You know what I'm guessing?" GAM asks. She smiles, as if to herself. "I think poor little Khufu is troubled. Where's his mother?"

"He doesn't have one. I mean, he said she moved away to New Mexico to be an artist. I don't even believe *that*."

GAM slowly shakes her head. "That's probably the one thing he's said that's true."

Gavin has to think about this. GAM might be right, and that gives him a funny feeling too. Still, Khufu can't just go around stealing another person's bike, spray-painting it an ugly orange, and pretending it's his.

Seven
More Big Whoppers

Good. *The weekend is almost here,* Gavin thinks as he gets out of his mother's car on Friday and waves good-bye. He looks toward the bike rack. His friends' bicycles are there. And there's the ugly orange bike. He'll have to get it professionally painted to cover that horrible color. When he gets it back.

● ● ●

"We're going to get Gavin's bike back tomorrow," Richard tells Carlos and Calvin as they walk toward the foursquare court at recess.

"Like I warned you, you could get caught by his *father,*" Carlos says. "And what if the bike is locked?"

"It isn't. He keeps it behind this big dumpster next to his building under a huge piece of cardboard," Richard informs them.

The group is quiet—thinking.

Then the lineup bell rings, and everyone on the playground hurries to their assigned places on the schoolyard.

● ● ●

During social studies, Ms. Shelby-Ortiz talks about timelines—personal timelines and how everyone has one. To show what she means, she draws a line on

the board and turns to the class with a sly smile as if she's about to let them in on a secret. She directs her question to Khufu. "Khufu, can we use your information for our timeline?"

Khufu smiles broadly. "Sure," he says.

Ms. Shelby-Ortiz asks him his birth date, and Khufu tells her. The class grows momentarily quiet as they are busy figuring out if they're older or younger than he is.

"Birthplace?" Ms. Shelby-Ortiz asks.

"Sweden," he says.

Ms. Shelby-Ortiz starts to write that down but stops. "Oh . . . right. Sweden," she says slowly.

"Yes," says Khufu simply.

"How did it happen that you were born in Sweden?" It doesn't sound as if she doesn't believe him. She just sounds curious.

"My family was traveling there for a reason that's secret. So I can't tell you why."

"And how long did you live in *Sweden?*"

"Until I was five."

"So, then, do you speak Swedish?" Antonia butts in. She rolls her eyes. She clearly doesn't believe him.

"Of course I speak Swedish," Khufu says, not sounding the least bit worried that he might be tested.

"Say something, then."

Ms. Shelby-Ortiz watches this exchange as if she, too, wants Khufu to say something in Swedish.

Khufu continues to look perfectly calm. In fact, he stands up as if he's ready to meet any challenge and he's going to speak paragraphs and paragraphs and silence his doubters.

"Say your name and tell us if you have any brothers and sisters," Deja blurts out.

Khufu smiles as if that's a super-easy challenge—one he can meet without even trying. He takes in a big breath, and a stream of gobbledygook comes out of his mouth. Gavin's eyes widen, and he glances around. Kids are looking at one another either with a laugh bubbling up or their mouths hanging open in disbelief. Even Ms. Shelby-Ortiz looks down as if she doesn't want anyone to see her trying not to laugh. Finally she asks, "And you lived there how long, again?"

Khufu sighs. "I came to this country when I was five. Like I said."

"Could you speak English?" Ralph calls out.

"I had to learn English when I got here."

"How come you don't have an accent?" Deja challenges.

Khufu turns to her and says evenly, "I did have an accent, but I got rid of it."

Ms. Shelby-Ortiz claps her hands together once. "Let's move on," she says.

Gavin can tell most of the kids in Room Ten don't want to move on from their line of questioning. He guesses there are plenty who have many more questions they'd like to put to Khufu.

Finally, a detailed timeline is on the board, depicting Khufu's life from his birth—in Sweden—until the day he showed up at Carver Elementary School.

But before paper is passed out so that everyone can create their own timeline, Khufu adds one more bit of information.

"Another thing," he says. "It just so happens I'm part Native American. And we no longer find it offensive to be called Indians. And that's why I wear the braids—because I'm part Indian."

Now all the girls stare at him—and his braids.

Again Ms. Shelby-Ortiz looks down as if to hide

what she's thinking. She has Nikki pass out the 8½ x 14 inch paper so the rest of the class can get started. Gavin can't help glancing over at Khufu's paper from time to time, and sees the most fantastical events suddenly included. *When he was six, he climbed Mount Everest with his father?* Gavin knows about Mount Everest and it being the tallest mountain on earth. Who would believe such a big whopper? Gavin checks Khufu's face. He's wearing a self-satisfied smile as he continues to record huge milestones. *When he was six and a half, he performed opera at . . .* Gavin can't make out the rest.

That settles it. Khufu stole the bike. Anyone who can tell such big fibs must also be able to take what doesn't belong to him. Finally Gavin is sure.

● ● ●

There it is again—the orange bicycle. *His* bicycle in the bicycle rack, put there by Khufu. Gavin stares at it for a few moments until he hears the bell ring, signaling the end of recess. He sighs and heads to Room Ten's area on the yard. Soon Richard and Calvin and Carlos join him. Before they know it, Ms. Shelby-Ortiz is crossing to where they stand waiting, her clipboard in hand. She doesn't bring her clipboard every time. You never know when she'll bring it and begin making notes of their behavior. Are they standing quietly in line—keeping their hands to themselves, standing in the space she's assigned them? This is the time to earn points or lose them for a chance to reach into Ms. Shelby-Ortiz's grab bag at the end of the month and choose a prize. And it's not just pencils and erasers she's got in that bag. There are markers and Hot Wheels and diaries for the girls and Slinkys and lots of other good stuff.

● ● ●

The day hums along. Gavin occasionally sneaks a peek at Khufu as he does his work. He looks so pleased with himself. He always finishes in record time and then pulls a book out of his desk to read for pleasure. Gavin glances at the title: *The Seven Deadliest Animals on Earth*. He frowns. On the page is something called a

Cape buffalo, with giant horns. Then there's a jelly-fish with deadly-looking tentacles waving in the water. Khufu gazes at the picture and the warning to seek medical help as quickly as possible if stung.

Gavin shudders. He's curious and fearful at the same time.

When the dismissal bell rings, Ms. Shelby-Ortiz calls on Gavin's table to be the first to line up. To add insult to injury, Khufu goes directly to his cubby and takes out a brand-new bicycle helmet. He puts it on and adjusts the chin strap.

When Ms. Shelby-Ortiz notices, she goes on and on about how she's so happy to see Khufu showing responsibility in choosing to wear a bicycle helmet, and how important it is to understand the necessity of it. She doesn't know how many times she's seen kids on bikes with no helmets. Which makes her wonder about their parents. "Everyone, a helmet is essential in protecting your head from injury. I don't want to see anyone on a bicycle without one." But then she turns to Khufu and says quietly, "You don't have to put it on now. You can wait until you're getting on your bike."

Khufu, still wearing his new helmet, and the rest of Table Two walk out of the classroom silent and straight, like soldiers. But once outside, they run in all different directions, some whooping and hollering just because they can. Khufu, however, goes directly to Gavin's bike spray-painted orange and hops on. Gavin watches him ride away.

● ● ●

"Mom," Gavin says as they walk through the front door, "did you decide if I can spend the night at Richard's tonight?"

Danielle, sauntering by on her way to the kitchen, squints at him suspiciously. "Why?" she asks. "Why do you want to spend the night at Richard's?"

"Because he invited me."

"What about your chores? Your Saturday chores?"

"I can do them when I get home."

That's when GAM chimes in. She's now spending more time downstairs in Gavin's father's big recliner in the family room, catching up on her soap operas.

"And what business is it of yours?" she calls to Danielle over her shoulder.

Danielle suddenly seems flustered. Gavin's mother

smiles to herself. If she had asked Danielle that question, there would have been an argument. But Danielle would never argue with Aunt Myrtle.

"I need to speak to Richard's mother and see if it's all right," Gavin's mother says, which means the answer isn't quite yes—yet. But it's leaning toward yes.

● ● ●

It's a miracle that Richard's mom agrees, because instead of four loud boys, she's now going to have four loud boys plus a fifth slightly—at times—loud boy. Gavin and his mom get into the car, but before starting for Richard's, she goes through the sleepover rules once again: No loud, raucous play in the house; adults must be addressed as *Mr.* and *Ms.* (Gavin doesn't get that one. *Everybody* calls adults by their first names. Most times adults introduce *themselves* by their first names.); absolutely no going into the refrigerator or kitchen cabinets—even with permission from Richard; put away all toys, clothes, and the sleeping bag when not in use. Don't be a guest people hate to see coming. Be a guest people *like* to see coming. Gavin knows all this already. He just wishes his mother would start the car so he can hurry up and get to Richard's.

Eight
The Return of the Bike

When Gavin and his mother arrive at Richard's house, everyone is in the backyard playing basketball: Richard's father; his brother Darnell, who's in the fifth grade at Carver Elementary; his brother Jamal, who's in middle school; and his oldest brother, Roland, who's in high school. *Why can't I exchange Danielle for three brothers?* Gavin wonders. That would be great. Too bad he can't just make a trade.

Gavin joins in, and the game is so intense and so much fun that he forgets why he's spending the night there in the first place.

By the time they go inside, Richard's mom has pizza waiting. Three large pizzas. They sit at the dining room table, and no one has to look at the last piece of pizza and wonder who'll be able to grab it first. There's plenty. Everyone's eventually full.

● ● ●

"Get up, Gavin. We have to do this quick."

At first Gavin doesn't know where he is. He looks around and remembers. *Oh, yeah*. He gets dressed in no time. Then he's ready to go.

They slip out the back door. "It's really not that far," Richard whispers, leading the way.

Richard's block is deserted. A pickup truck suddenly turns down the street and slows in front of the house next door. It stops. A man gets out, stands at the end of the walkway, and tosses a folded newspaper onto the porch. He looks at Richard and Gavin with what seems to be a puzzled look on his face. The sun is barely up. He must be wondering where two boys could be going at such an early hour. It's a little strange being out on his own with Richard. He's gone to the park with just a friend or two and no adults, but this feels different.

"Come on," Richard says. "We have to hurry."

● ● ●

It turns out the apartment where Khufu lives is also not far from the park. In fact, Gavin has passed his building many times before. The street is quiet. Gavin and Richard glance around to make sure no one is watching them. They round the side of the building to where the trash bin is located. The bike is easy to see, even though it's almost hidden by a big flat piece of cardboard with a fold in the middle.

"Why doesn't he just keep it in his apartment?" Gavin wonders out loud.

"Maybe his father doesn't even know about the bike! Yeah, how could he just bring a bike home?" Richard chuckles. "'Hey, Dad . . . look what I found'?"

"But then where did he get the orange spray paint?"

"Maybe he already had it," Richard says. "Maybe he's one of those kids who's always tagging stuff."

● ● ●

Richard yanks off the cardboard, and they both stare at the orange bike for a few seconds. Then Richard pushes up the kickstand with his foot and hurriedly walks the bicycle out of the alley and down the street with Gavin close behind. Gavin stares at the bike. He wants to ride it, but Richard is on foot, so Gavin will have to wait until he's on his way home.

As soon as they get back to Richard's house, Richard puts the orange bicycle in his backyard. Gavin can figure out what to do later. He needs time to decide what he's going to tell his parents. They might not like the idea of him just sneaking over to Khufu's and taking his bike back. Without permission.

Richard and Gavin slip into the house through the back door. Richard gets the box of cinnamon cereal and two bowls out of the cabinet. He pours some cereal into them. He gets the milk out of the refrigerator and hands it to Gavin. Gavin pours milk over his cereal and digs in. He hasn't realized until that moment that he's starving. Richard must be too, because for a while, neither of them says a word. The cinnamon cereal tastes great.

"Let's ride our bikes to the park later," Richard suggests.

"I have to go home first and get my chores out of the way."

"How long will that take?"

"Couple of hours."

Richard rolls his eyes. "Okay. I'll call Carlos and Calvin and see if they can meet us."

● ● ●

Everything feels a little off to Gavin. He can't put his finger on it. And it's not just that Roland's helmet, which he lent to Gavin for the ride home, doesn't fit quite right. It's something about the bicycle's seat. It doesn't feel familiar. And are the handlebars a little bit higher than he remembers? He shakes his head. It's probably just his imagination.

When Gavin reaches his house, it's still early enough to walk the bike around to the backyard and not be noticed. He hides it behind the toolshed as quietly as possible. He can't believe how easy it was—to get his bike back. Of course, his mother and father might not see it that way. They might think it wasn't such a good idea to go to Khufu's house and just, well, *steal* the bike back.

Suddenly it occurs to him that he can't meet his

friends at the park to go bike riding. He's not going to be able to bring that bicycle out into the open until he explains things to his parents. It's his bike, but his parents aren't going to like the way he got it.

Gavin starts on his chores with his head full of heavy thoughts. While he sweeps the front porch, his mind goes to the orange bike behind the toolshed—and the funny feel of the seat. Maybe Khufu's weight did something to it. No, that isn't very likely. Khufu is just a skinny little kid. His weight wouldn't have done anything.

But it's more than that. The bike just doesn't feel like the bike he remembers. There's something else that's different.

"What are you doing?" It's Danielle, standing in the doorway with a blueberry muffin in her hand. And he'd thought all the muffins were gone. He'd specifically looked for the package as soon as he got home.

"Where did you get that muffin? I thought they were all gone."

"Ha! Wouldn't you like to know?"

"Are you hiding muffins in your bedroom?"

Danielle ignores the question and gets back to the subject at hand. "You're just standing there with the broom and a funny look on your face. What's going on?"

"Nothing. I was just thinking about something."

"You, thinking?" She laughs, takes a big bite out of her muffin, and goes back inside.

As soon as Gavin finishes the porch, he makes a trip to the back of the toolshed to look at his bike. It's still there. But what good is a bicycle if you can't ride it? He can't ride it to school. Khufu would claim that it belongs to him. He can't ride it to the park, because he hasn't told his parents about going to Khufu's and "stealing" it back. The bike just has to sit there, *unrideable,* until he can straighten everything out.

Gavin sighs. Now it's time to tackle his bedroom: dust; change the linens; clean under the bed; vacuum. Oh, the misery of Saturday chores.

●●●

"Pass the mashed potatoes, please," Danielle says. She smiles politely at Gavin, and he immediately wonders what's up. Danielle is only super polite when she's about to do him in somehow. He frowns and passes the potatoes.

"And then pass them this way," says his father.

Everyone is at the dining room table for dinner, even Aunt Myrtle. She's feeling much better and will probably be in great shape when Uncle Vestor comes to pick her up in three or four days—after his conference is over. Something occurs to Gavin then. Something so bizarre, he almost pushes it out of his head. Does Uncle Vestor just make up these conferences so he can get away? Maybe go fishing with his buddies?

Actually, it doesn't matter, because this time, Gavin has actually enjoyed having GAM at his house. He's appreciated her

take on the whole bike thing. Even though it's put a small doubt in his mind.

"Gavin," Danielle pipes up, "do you plan to try to save up for a new bike?"

"I'll be saving for the next ten years," Gavin says.

His mother smiles. "Well, at least we'll know what to get him for his *next* birthday."

"Tell you what," his father says. "I'll match every dollar you save, and that way you'll be able to replace the bike quicker. It won't seem so impossible."

Gavin thinks. He does still have some birthday money. But then he shakes himself out of it. He's forgotten already. He *has* a bicycle. It's behind the toolshed. He just needs to let his parents in on what he did: that he took his bike back, since he is the rightful owner. If he puts it that way, they just might understand.

His thoughts are interrupted by Danielle's voice. "But what about that orange bike you've got hidden behind the toolshed?"

All heads turn toward Gavin. He stops breathing. GAM is frowning. There also seems to be a look of disappointment in her eyes. Perhaps she thought he wouldn't go through with the scheme he and his friends cooked up.

"What's Danielle talking about?" his mother asks. Both his mother and his father wait for him to answer.

Gavin studies his mound of peas. When he glances up, his parents are still looking at him and waiting.

"I found out who stole my bike," Gavin tells them.

"What?" his mother and father say at the same time.

"It was this new kid, Khufu. He took my bike."

"How do you know this?" his mother asks.

Danielle is leaning back in her chair with her arms crossed. "Yeah," she adds. "How do you *know* this kid took your bike?"

Gavin is ready with his list. "Number one, the day my bike was stolen, he left school early. He said he had a dentist appointment, but I don't believe that. I think he changed the time on his appointment slip so he could leave early and take my bike."

"That's kind of a stretch," his father says.

"Yeah—a stretch," Danielle agrees.

Gavin scowls at her and goes on. "Then the next day, there was this bike in the bike rack that looked like it was spray-painted this ugly orange to hide the real color. Which I think was silver and blue, the color of my bike. And it had the same spokes and the same seat and it was the same size. And it was a BMX like my bike. Plus it was Khufu who brought that bike to school. *My* bike."

His mother and father are looking at him as if they're having some trouble following all of this.

"So you stole the bike back?" his mother asks.

"I don't think it's stealing if it's my bike in the first place."

"You don't *know* that," his mother says. GAM nods slowly.

Gavin is quiet.

"I want you to think about this," his father says. "Finish your dinner. I need you to show me what makes you certain that that bike is yours. Whatever the case may be, we—your mother and I—need to talk to this boy's parents."

"He only has a father," Gavin says, more to himself than to anyone else.

● ● ●

After dinner, Gavin, his father, his mother, and of course Danielle traipse out to the back of the toolshed to study the orange bicycle. Gavin's father wheels it to the light of the back porch. He lowers the kickstand so the bike can be upright on its own under the light. All four of them stare at it.

"It does look like it was spray-painted this color," his father says.

"And it's a BMX and it's the same size as mine," Gavin adds.

"Still, that doesn't mean it's your bike," his mother counters.

"He could have just wanted a bike that color," Danielle says.

Gavin glares at her. Why is she rooting for the person who stole his bike?

"Then he could have just gotten an orange bicycle," his mother says.

Danielle opens her mouth, but their father's voice cuts her off.

"We're going to think this thing through. Meanwhile, no riding that bike until we get a chance to speak to this Khufu person's parents."

"He lives with just his father."

"You have his telephone number?" his father asks.

"No. I can get it on Monday."

His father sighs. "I don't feel comfortable waiting until Monday to settle this. Get your jacket, Gavin. You know where he lives. We can take care of this now."

"Wait until Monday," Gavin's mother says. "Then you'll have time to think of the best way to approach this situation."

His father seems to be thinking about her suggestion. Finally, he says, "Okay, Monday."

Nine
The Awful Thing That Happened

On Monday, the students from Room Ten are lined up in their assigned area when Gavin sees Khufu slowly crossing the yard. Gavin, Richard, Carlos, and Calvin glance at one another. There's something about the slump of Khufu's shoulders and the slowness of his gait that lets them know that he has discovered "his" bike is gone. Gavin and his friends exchange glances again.

Khufu joins the line and stands there motionless. Usually he has a book in his hand that he opens up to read while everyone waits for Ms. Shelby-Ortiz. This time he just stares ahead blankly. When Ms. Shelby-Ortiz arrives to lead them to the classroom, Antonia, who's standing behind Khufu, has to nudge him to get moving.

Once in Room Ten, he puts his things away in his cubby, goes to his desk, sinks into his chair, and sits there looking as if he's in his own world. Gavin finishes up at his cubby and takes his seat. He checks the morning journal topic, happy to see that it's open. Gavin's relieved. They usually have to write about their weekend on Monday mornings. Maybe Ms. Shelby-Ortiz forgot. He wants to write about his stolen bicycle again. How it felt to get it back. He plans to leave out the part about taking it back from Khufu.

As usual, Khufu has dived in and is writing in his journal nonstop. Gavin sneaks a glance and almost feels sorry for him. As usual, Khufu seems to have a lot to say. He continues even after Ms. Shelby-Ortiz calls time. "Pencils down," she says. Then, "You know—we haven't had any sharing in a while. Is there someone who'd like to share their journal entry?"

Khufu's hand shoots up. Ms. Shelby-Ortiz looks a bit surprised. Khufu has such a determined look on his face, she probably feels she has to pick him.

"Okay," she says. "You may share yours, Khufu."

Some kids are talking, and Khufu stands and

waits with his mouth zipped. He looks as if he would waits a year if need be.

"All mouths closed and give Khufu your undivided attention," Ms. Shelby-Ortiz says.

When they are finally quiet, he begins:

"Dear Morning Journal, on Saturday, I experienced the worst day of my life."

Everyone stops their fidgeting and turns toward Khufu to *really* give him their undivided attention.

"I have to back up. See, I always wanted a bike, but there never was enough money for me to get one. I live in a tiny studio apartment with my father. He does odd jobs, so there's only enough money for food and shelter. Last week was my birthday, and my father surprised me with a used BMX bike. I was so, so happy. There was just one problem. It was pink. Because it was a girl's bike. And it belonged to our neighbor's daughter, who's a grownup now. Or she's in high school. I was happy anyway, and my dad said he'd fix the color. He got some spray paint and painted it orange—which was not the best color, but that color was on sale."

Gavin begins to get a horrible sinking feeling.

"Now, let me tell you what it felt like when I was riding my bike. It felt like I was free. It felt like I was flying—and it felt like I could go anywhere in the world. So I was super happy.

I had to keep my bike behind the big trash bin and I had to hide it under some cardboard because our apartment is so small, the bike would have taken up too much space. On Saturday, my dad said I could ride my bike at the park, and I was so happy and was feeling so lucky. And I was happy that my father had gotten this good job at Simply Delicious Health Food Store. I went to get my bike from my hiding place . . ."

Khufu stops here, and it seems as if he's trying to keep from crying. Gavin's horrible, awful feeling is getting worse. He hopes that Khufu doesn't start to cry. He looks over at Richard, who's staring at his hands on his lap. Carlos is frowning, and Calvin is staring at Khufu with his lips parted and his eyes wide.

Finally, Khufu pulls himself together and continues. "It wasn't there. I searched the whole alley. My dad came down and helped me search. It was gone. Someone stole it. For that person, it was nothing. But for me, that bike was everything.

"Maybe when I grow up and get a job, I can get another bike. But it won't feel like my first bike. Even if it was once pink and my dad had to spray-paint it with paint he got on sale."

The class is quiet for a few seconds after Khufu finishes. Ms. Shelby-Ortiz is quiet too. It's as if everyone is thinking about what Khufu wrote. Then Deja starts waving her hand around until Ms. Shelby-Ortiz calls on her. "Deja?"

"What about that bar thing that boys' bikes have? People would still know that it's not a boy bike without that bar thing."

Khufu looks at her for a few seconds. "It had the bar thing. The only reason why girls' bikes were different in the past was because girls wore dresses.

Bikes without bars accommodated girls who wore dresses. Girls don't wear dresses as much now."

Rosario's hand shoots up and she waves it around until Ms. Shelby-Ortiz calls on her. "Ms. Shelby-Ortiz, I happen to think that horrible person who stole Khufu's bike should be put in jail. I think that person who took your bike, Khufu, is the most horrible person who ever lived." At this point her voice cracks, and Gavin thinks she might just cry as well. He swallows.

Richard looks over at Gavin, his eyes wide. He notices Carlos and Calvin looking over at him too.

Khufu sits down, and Ms. Shelby-Ortiz walks over to him and puts her hand on his shoulder. "I'm so, so sorry that happened to you."

Khufu just stares straight ahead.

● ● ●

"What should we do?" Carlos says to Gavin at recess. Gavin's friends have gathered at the four-square court, but nobody's playing.

"We have to give it back," Gavin says.

"But maybe it's not Khufu's bike," Richard counters. "He could be telling a big story. You know how he lies."

Gavin shakes his head. "I don't think he's telling a fib in this case."

● ● ●

It isn't until Gavin is walking to his mother's car that he remembers he didn't get Khufu's number. In a way, he did that on purpose. Khufu would wonder why he wanted his telephone number, and what could Gavin say? That he's the one who took Khufu's bike, thinking it was his own?

"Did you get the number?" his mother asks.

"I forgot."

"Have fun explaining that to your father."

● ● ●

As soon as he gets home, Gavin goes directly to the toolshed. He pulls the bike out, stands it up, and studies it. He looks it over carefully. Could it have once been pink under that ugly orange? Could Khufu have just made up the whole thing about his father buying the used bike from a neighbor and that it was for his birthday?

Then he sees it. A small spot. A smudge, actually—where the orange paint looks thin.

He moves the bike so the spot is out in the sunlight. Pink. He sighs and feels his stomach drop. He *stole* Khufu's bicycle. He has to give it back. And he needs to do it as soon as possible.

But how?

Richard's coming over to play basketball later. Maybe he can go with him. After all, Richard kind of got him into this.

When Richard arrives, Gavin takes him around to the back of the toolshed to show him the spot where some of the pink color beneath the orange shows through. "Look," he says, pointing to it.

"What?" says Richard, squinting.

"You don't see the pink under the orange?"

Richard looks closer. "Maybe," he says after a while.

"Admit it, Richard. It's pink," Gavin insists.

Richard looks again. "I guess."

"We have to give it back."

"When?" Richard asks.

"Let's do it *now*. Wait for me out front. I have to get permission—and I have to get something."

Ten
Khufu's Dad

Gavin dashes inside to get permission from his mom and runs into his father coming through the front door.

"What's the hurry?" his father asks.

"I forgot to get Khufu's number, Dad. But I already know the orange bike is his." Gavin sighs.

"You're sure?" his father says, looking at him closely.

Gavin's face burns with shame and embarrassment. "Yes," he says in a small voice.

"Go return it, then," his father orders. "And apologize for jumping to conclusions and for taking something that didn't belong to you."

"Okay," Gavin says, and then he runs upstairs for the thing he has to get. Then he's off.

● ● ●

"I just thought of something," Richard says as they walk up to the rundown apartment building where Khufu lives. Gavin hadn't wanted to ride Khufu's bike, so Richard left his in Gavin's backyard. "We don't know which apartment he lives in."

Gavin leads the way up the front stairs and looks at the bank of doorbells. Each has a name beneath it, but "Grundy" isn't one of them. "I don't see Khufu's last name," Gavin says. "It's Grundy, right?"

"Yeah," Richard says.

"Well, they just moved here. Maybe they haven't gotten around to putting their name on their doorbell," Gavin reasons.

"There's only six," Richard points out. "Just ring them all."

Gavin shrugs.

No one answers the first bell. An old-sounding woman answers the second bell, but then she can't quite understand Gavin's question when he asks, "Does Khufu live there?"

"Who?" she says.

"Never mind," Gavin says.

He rings the third bell, and Khufu answers. "Who is it?" he says.

Gavin pauses. He feels self-conscious. "It's Gavin—and Richard," he blurts out.

"Gavin? And Richard?" Khufu sounds surprised.

"Yeah, and Richard."

"Oh."

There's a moment of silence.

"We brought you something."

More silence. Then, "What?"

"Your bike," Gavin says.

There's more silence. Gavin looks over his shoulder at Richard. They wait for Khufu to say something. Then they hear feet clomping down the stairs inside the building. Finally, the door swings open, and there stands Khufu in jeans and a T-shirt. He spies his bike, and his mouth drops open. Slowly, he comes down the front steps. He walks over to the bike that Richard is holding and runs his hand over the seat.

"I can't believe it," he says in a near whisper. "I can't believe it." He looks over at Richard and Gavin. "Where'd you find it?"

Suddenly Gavin feels scared. What is Khufu going to think when he tells him he was the one who stole it? Then the front door opens and a man who looks just like Khufu, only with a head full of long locks and an earring in one ear, steps out. "Who do we have here?"

Khufu looks up at him and says, "These are two of my classmates. They brought me my bike."

"I see. Thank you! Did you find out who took it?"

Gavin swallows hard. "Yes."

"Who?" Khufu's father asks, still wearing a smile.

"I took it," Gavin says.

"*We* took it," Richard adds.

Khufu's father frowns and cocks his head to the side. Khufu's mouth drops open.

Gavin isn't sure how to explain how they happen to have Khufu's bike. "We thought he had stolen the bike from me," he offers.

Khufu's father frowns even more and looks puzzled. The four of them just stand there. "Come inside, and you can explain everything to me," Khufu's dad finally says. Khufu takes the bike out of Richard's hands, then looks as if he doesn't know what to do with it.

"Oh," Gavin says. "I brought you this." He holds out his brand-new bicycle lock, the one he's never used. Khufu might as well have it. Gavin has no need for it now.

Khufu stares at it with surprise. "Thank you," he says quietly. He takes the lock and attaches the bike

to the railing next to the bottom step. They all go into the building.

○ ○ ○

Khufu's apartment is unusual. It's basically one room with a small kitchen area, two twin beds in the corners, a couch, and four tall bookshelves filled with books. Gavin and Richard stand in the middle of it and look around.

"Have a seat," Khufu's father says, "and start from the beginning."

Gavin tells about his bike going missing and a bike showing up in the bike rack the next day looking like it was painted to disguise it.

Khufu's father is actually smiling. "It was an easy mistake to make, I suppose," he says.

Gavin feels some relief. He decides right then and there that he likes Khufu's father. And he likes Khufu, too.

"So you're out of a bike," Khufu's dad observes.

"And my father says I'll have to save up to get a new one. But he said he'll match whatever I save, so I won't have to take such a long time."

"Well, that's something to look forward to, I guess," Khufu's father says.

● ● ●

On the walk home, Gavin is newly energized. "Let's get our skateboards and go to the park," he suggests to Richard when they get to his house.

Richard agrees. "Calvin and Carlos are going to be there. They said they felt like skateboarding today." Gavin breathes a sigh of relief. It's as if a weight has been lifted off his shoulders. He's back to having no bike, but the thought of trying out some new moves at the skate park fills his mind.

His father is on the couch watching golf when Gavin goes inside and starts for the stairs.

"Did you return the bike to its rightful owner?"

"Yes," Gavin says. He stands in the doorway. "And it all worked out. His father was real nice. And he was understanding, too. And I gave my lock to Khufu so he wouldn't have to hide his bike under a big piece of cardboard behind the dumpster in the back of his apartment building."

"That was nice of you," his father says.

Now Gavin feels extra good. He no longer feels like that horrible person Rosario was ready to have thrown in jail. He's back to feeling like himself.

○ ○ ○

GAM is proud of him too. She tells him so at the dinner table that night. "You see how you can be so sure of something and still be wrong?" she adds.

"Yeah, do you see?" Danielle repeats, then glances at Aunt Myrtle as if she suddenly wants to please her.

Aunt Myrtle looks at her with one raised eyebrow.

"I'm sure you're relieved," his mother ventures.

Gavin smiles, but then looks down at the pile of

mashed turnips on his plate. How is he ever going to get that mound of turnips down? He takes a tiny bite and nearly gags. He gulps down some milk. He's got about ten more bites. He hopes he has enough milk.

"You know what?" Aunt Myrtle says. Everyone looks at her. "I'm going to add to that match your father has promised. I'll match what he matches."

Gavin doesn't exactly know what that adds up to, but it sounds like a good thing. "Thank you, GA—I mean, Aunt Myrtle."

"You'll have enough money for a new bike in no time."

Eleven
Mystery Solved

As soon as Gavin climbs out of his mother's car and makes it to the lineup area the next morning, Deja marches up to him and says, "I hear you're the one who stole Khufu's bike."

"Yeah," Rosario says, joining her. "How could you do something like that to Khufu?"

Gavin opens his mouth to speak. First of all—how did she hear that? Maybe Khufu told her, not realizing how Deja would take it. Richard comes over and quickly chimes in. "I helped him take the bike, and we only took it because Gavin's bike got stolen and he thought Khufu was the thief."

"Why didn't you just ask him?" Deja asks.

Calvin walks up then. "How's it your business?" he asks.

"Yeah," Richard agrees. "Anyway, as soon as he found out the bike really was Khufu's, he gave it back. So mind your own business."

Deja starts to say something, but then quickly turns and gets in line. Ms. Shelby-Ortiz is coming—with her clipboard.

Their teacher marches the class to Room Ten. She

has them remain in line just outside the classroom door until she feels they are ready to enter quietly. Some have started to talk and fidget.

When everyone has settled down, she steps aside. The class enters. Some go to their cubbies to put away their backpacks; some get to hang their backpacks on their chairs. Gavin watches his friends put their bike helmets in their cubbies. He sighs. He supposes he'll just have to feel this way—sad and disappointed— for the rest of the school year . . . until he can save enough for a new bike.

As soon as everyone is seated and pulling out their morning journals, Rosario's hand shoots up.

Ms. Shelby-Ortiz looks up from the clipboard and calls on her.

"Ms. Shelby-Ortiz, we know who stole Khufu's bike!" Rosario looks over at Gavin, appearing happy and excited to report this.

Gavin feels his heart drop.

Before their teacher can say anything, Rosario blurts it out. "Gavin's the one who stole Khufu's bike, Ms. Shelby-Ortiz!"

"What?" Ms. Shelby-Ortiz turns to Gavin with a puzzled look on her face. "Is that true, Gavin?"

"Yes, but only because I thought the bike was mine."

Ms. Shelby-Ortiz shakes her head. "I'm not getting this."

"See, I got my bike stolen, and when Khufu

brought his bike to school, it looked a lot like mine, only orange, but I could see that that color was spray-painted over another color, so I thought the bike was mine." He takes a big breath.

"Couldn't you have just asked Khufu about his bike?"

"I didn't think he'd tell the truth, because . . ." Gavin stops then and looks over at Khufu. "Well, because."

Deja cuts in. "Because sometimes he doesn't tell the truth, Ms. Shelby-Ortiz. Like when he said he could speak Swedish, and that didn't sound like real Swedish to me."

Ms. Shelby-Ortiz interrupts her. "Uh—we don't know that. None of us speaks Swedish, so let's not accuse Khufu of not being truthful."

Khufu looks a little shifty-eyed as he lowers his head a bit.

"And then the genius school, Ms. Shelby-Ortiz," Antonia adds. "No one's ever really heard of a genius school." She looks over at Khufu with interest. He's busy picking at a fingernail.

Their teacher sighs. "Enough of this talk. Let's get to work." She claps her hands once. "Well, I'm glad everything is straightened out. And I'm sorry your bike was stolen, Gavin. Maybe you'll get another one. Let's hope. Now it's time to get to our morning journals."

● ● ●

Once again, Gavin's mother is waiting for him as he hauls himself down the front school steps. She waves happily, and he knows that she's trying to put him in a better mood.

The drive home is quiet. As soon as they pull into the driveway, Gavin gets out and slumps up the back steps and into the kitchen. He washes his hands at the sink and opens the refrigerator to stare into it. Nothing appeals to him. He closes the refrigerator door and goes over to the cabinet that holds snack food.

"Ah-ah-ah," his mother says behind him. "Get an apple."

Gavin sighs. Can things get much worse?

● ● ●

He's still in a bad mood at the dinner table that night. Happily, there's nothing on the table that's gag-worthy. Corn on the cob, baked chicken, and green beans. Well, he might have some problems with the green beans.

Danielle is busy trying to weasel permission out of their mother to spend the night at her best friend's house on Saturday. Gavin's rooting for his mom to give permission. An evening without Danielle in the house sounds like heaven.

Just as his mother opens her mouth to ask her usual series of questions, the doorbell rings. Everyone looks at one another. His father frowns and gets up to answer it.

Soon Gavin hears a man's voice sounding as if he's explaining something. He hears his father saying "Uh-huh" over and over. Then his father makes a sound of surprise. "Gavin, can you come in here, please?" he calls.

Danielle, not to be left out of the loop, follows. The front door is open, and there stands a strange man—with Gavin's bike! Gavin's silver-and-blue BMX! He cannot believe his eyes! Is that really his bike?

"My bike . . ." Gavin manages in a hushed voice.

"Do you mind telling my son what you just told me?" his father asks.

"Sure," the man says. "So, I'm Robert Turner's father." He reaches out and shakes Gavin's hand.

Gavin knows who Robert Turner is. He's a boy in the fifth grade. He's in Gregory Johnson's class.

"As you can see, I've got your bike."

Gavin's father smiles.

"Let me explain," Robert Turner's dad goes on. "Last week, my wife got a call from the school telling her that Robert was in the nurse's office with flu symptoms. She dashed to the school, picked him up, and took him directly to the doctor. And he did have the flu. He's home in bed as we speak."

Gavin looks at his father and the big grin on his face.

"I came home early and assumed Robert had ridden his bike to school that day, so I swung by the school and picked up the bike and put it in the garage where it belongs. Or so I thought.

"Robert always leaves his bike in the backyard, and I'm always telling him that he needs to put it away in the garage or at least remember to lock it up and—well, never mind all that. Anyway, I thought the bike I put in the garage was his, but his bike was leaning against the back steps the whole time. Today I discovered the bike in the garage was *not his bike*." Mr. Turner slapped his forehead. "Robert knew just who it belonged to. His friend—whose little brother is in your class—told him whose it was." He turns to Gavin and says with a smile, "Have you been missing a bike?"

Gavin is so overcome, he's almost speechless. Now he knows exactly how Khufu felt when they returned his bike to him. Finally, he says, "Yes. I thought someone stole it."

Robert's father laughs. "I guess that someone was me. Though I didn't know that's what I was doing—walking off with someone else's bicycle."

Gavin moves to his bike and runs his hand along

the handlebars. He looks at his father. "I don't have to save for a new bike now."

"It looks that way," his father agrees.

"I just have to save up for a new lock."

His mother and GAM suddenly appear in the doorway next to Danielle and gaze at the bike, speechless.

Finally, GAM asks, "Is that your stolen bike?"

"It wasn't stolen," Gavin says.

"There was a bit of a mix-up," his father adds.

His dad and Mr. Turner shake hands again, and then the man turns toward his car.

"Who was that?" Gavin's mother asks.

"A parent who accidentally took Gavin's bike, thinking it belonged to his son."

"Wow," Danielle says. "What a mix-up." And it's a funny thing—she actually doesn't sound like her usual snide self. For once.

Gavin wheels his bike around the side of the house

and hauls it up the steps of the back porch. He puts the kickstand down and then steps away and looks at it. His bike has been *returned!* He almost can't believe it. He grins a big grin and then abruptly stops. He still has to get those green beans down.

Danielle sticks her head out the door. "You riding your bike to school tomorrow?"

"Not until I get a lock."

"You coming in?"

"In a minute."

He'll get back to those beans soon enough. For now, he just wants to enjoy sitting next to his silver-and-blue bicycle and thinking about when he'll get to ride it again.

The next book in the Carver Chronicles series is available now!

Third-grader Richard and his friends are just four days away from setting a record for excellent behavior and earning a classroom pizza party when disaster strikes—their beloved teacher is out sick, and the strictest, meanest substitute has taken her place! Will their dreams of pizza be dashed when the sub suspects that some of them have been cheating?